First published in Great Britain in 1980 by Andersen Press Ltd.,
20 Vauxhall Bridge Road, London SW1V 2SA.
Published in Australia by Random House Australia Pty.,
20 Alfred Street, Milsons Point, Sydney, NSW 2061.
This mini edition first published by Andersen Press in 2005.
All rights reserved.
Colour separated in Switzerland by Photolitho AG, Zürich.
Printed and bound in Singapore by Tien Wah Press.

10   9   8   7   6   5   4   3   2

British Library Cataloguing in Publication Data available.

ISBN 1 84270 456 7

This paper is made from wood pulp from sustainable forests

NOT NOW, BERNARD

David McKee

Ⓐ

Andersen Press
LONDON

"Hello, Dad," said Bernard.

"Not now, Bernard," said his father.

"Hello, Mum," said Bernard.

"Not now, Bernard," said his mother.

"There's a monster in the garden and it's going to eat me," said Bernard.

"Not now, Bernard," said his mother.

Bernard went into the garden.

"Hello, monster," he said
to the monster.

The monster ate Bernard up,
every bit.

Then the monster went indoors.

"ROAR," went the monster behind
Bernard's mother.

"Not now, Bernard,"
said Bernard's mother.

The monster bit Bernard's father.

"Not now, Bernard," said
Bernard's father.

"Your dinner's ready," said
Bernard's mother.

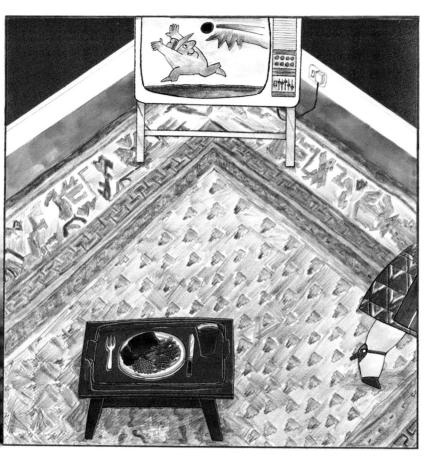

She put the dinner in front
of the television.

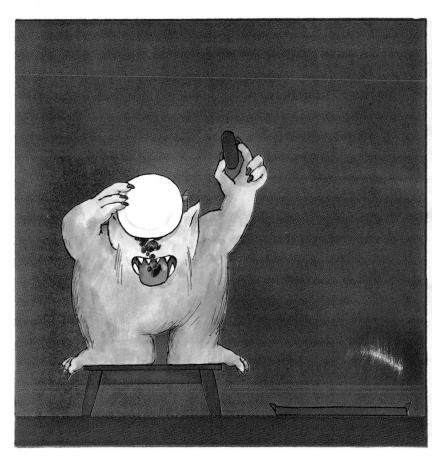

The monster ate the dinner.

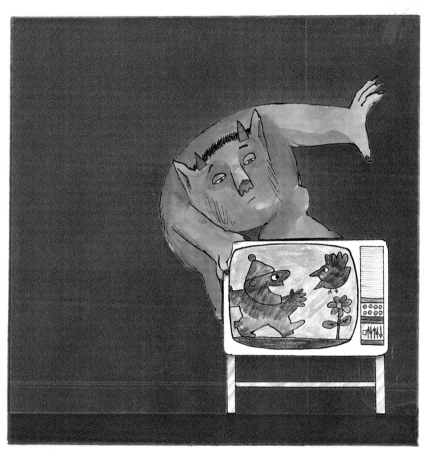

Then it watched the television.

Then it read one of Bernard's comics.

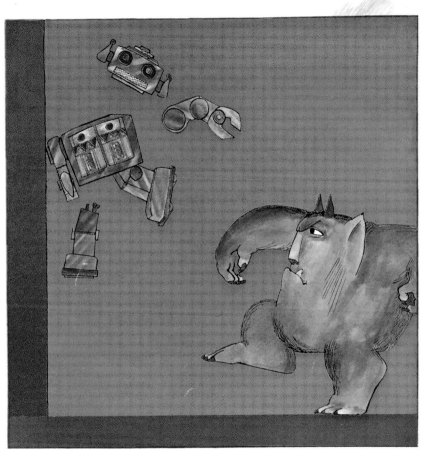

And broke one of his toys.

"Go to bed. I've taken up your milk,"
called Bernard's mother.

The monster went upstairs.

"But I'm a monster," said
the monster.

"Not now, Bernard,"
said Bernard's mother.